The Wedding Ghost

LEON GARFIELD/CHARLES KEEPING

OXFORD UNIVERSITY PRESS

OXFORD TORONTO MELBOURNE

Oxford University Press, Walton Street, Oxford OX2 6DP

Oxford New York Toronto
Delhi Bombay Calcutta Madras Karachi
Petaling Jaya Singapore Hong Kong Tokyo
Nairobi Dar es Salaam Cape Town
Melbourne Auckland

and associated companies in
Berlin Ibadan

Oxford is a trade mark of Oxford University Press

Text © Leon Garfield 1985
Illustrations © Charles Keeping, 1985

First published 1985
Reprinted 1988, 1992

First published in paperback 1992

British Library Cataloguing in Publication Data
Garfield, Leon
The Wedding Ghost
I. Title
823′.914[J] PZ7
ISBN 0-19-279779-4 Hardback
ISBN 0-19-272246 8 Paperback

Typeset by Tradespools Ltd, Frome, Somerset
Printed in Hong Kong

To Nicholas Bawden

O mistress mine! where are you roaming?
O! stay and hear; your true love's coming.
That can sing both high and low.
Trip no further, pretty sweeting;
Journeys end in lovers meeting,
Every wise man's son doth know.

What is love? 'tis not hereafter;
Present mirth hath present laughter.
What's to come is still unsure:
In delay there lies no plenty;
Then come kiss me, sweet and twenty,
Youth's a stuff will not endure.

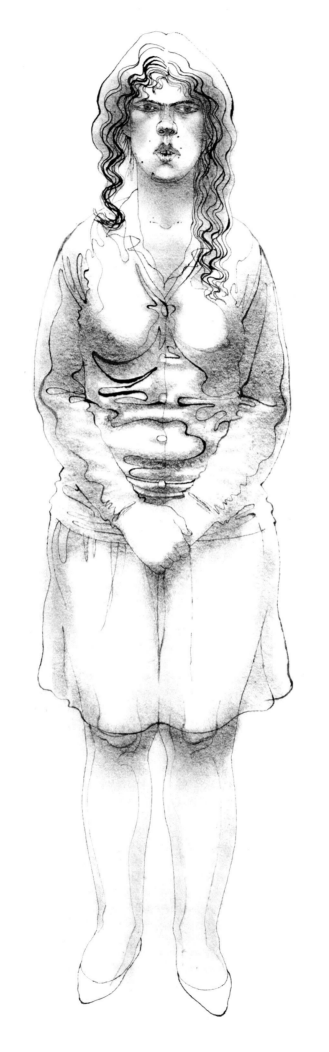

TIME snored, like Uncle Goodman after dinner; then woke up with a start. Glared in the glass, so to speak, and with a frantic look seemed to cry out: 'Good God! There's so little of me left!'

Then days rushed helter-skelter: mornings and afternoons leaping over one another, and nights tumbled anyhow in between. Visits to the tailor, the hatter, the haberdasher, for striped trousers, grey gloves, top hat, and a lavender coat with a tail, like a stork with the O.B.E. Then off to the florist's, with their green-coated girls with ferny smiles, for two dozen carnations in silver socks.

A wedding was in the air. In silver whispers on top quality card (that you had to tilt sideways to read) Mr and Mrs Goodman, of Oaklands, Little Mountwell, Herts, cordially requested the pleasure of the world and his wife's company (with but one trifling exception) on the occasion of the marriage of Gillian, their wondrous daughter, to Jack, one and only son of Samuel Best the Builders' Merchant (why go elsewhere when we are Best!)

4

at half-past twelve next Sunday, in the village church. R.S.V.P.

The world and his wife were coming; though God knew how they'd all squeeze into the church ... let alone into the house for the champagne buffet afterwards!

They'd all answered, every last one, from Brighton to Newark-on-Trent; except, of course, for the one who hadn't been invited, and she was only Jack's old nurse, who'd really been the maid. She'd long ago retired and lived so far away that it would have been an unkindness to have asked her and expected her to pay her fare and bring a gift besides.

Already it was Tuesday afternoon. The sky was a clerical grey, and soft mists obscured the fields and trees, like a ghostly bridal veil. The Goodmans' house, winking and gleaming in the dusk, was alive with the murmur of voices, the clinking of glasses and bursts of cheerful laughter. The wedding-rehearsal was over — strange, shuffling make-believe, in plain, dull clothes, in a plain, dull church, with the organ playing Handel's *Water Music*, and

5

Uncle Goodman loudly wondering if Handel wrote anything for whisky or gin – and everyone was settled in the Goodmans' comfortable front room.

The time had come for the opening of the presents. There was a November wind in the chimney and a blazing fire in the hearth, that roasted your back and made bright little ovens in Jill's wide eyes; and on the sideboard, for all to gasp at, was a king's ransom of teapots, cream jugs, biscuit barrels, pastry forks, lace table-cloths, and pale green sheets piled up like enormous cucumber sandwiches. And still there was more to come!

'A toast! A toast! ... A toast-rack!'

Down went the sherry, though it was only half-past four; and up came a toast-rack, trailing wisps of tissue-paper. On to the sideboard it went, where it joined two shining sisters, in a tangle of silver ribs, like a Museum of Unnatural History.

'No changing your mind now, my boy!' warned Uncle Goodman, wagging a large, pink finger. 'You'd have to send everything back!'

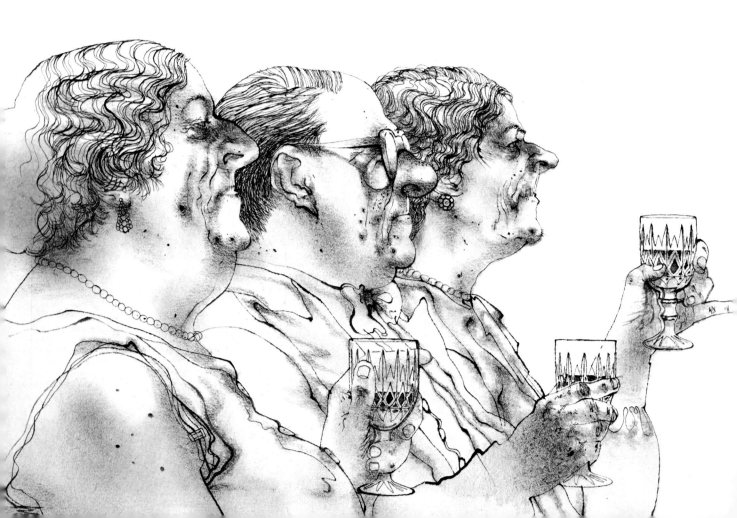

'Wouldn't dream of it, sir,' protested Jack, never at a loss for a humorous reply. 'It would cost a fortune in stamps!'

Everybody laughed, and Jack beamed with pride at having come off so well in the battle of wits; while Jill, sitting like a mermaid in a tumbled tide of boxes and brown paper, looked as if she wished him and Uncle Goodman at the bottom of the sea. Her price ought to have been far above rubies, not just cheaper than a few stamps!

A portly, rosy man was Uncle Goodman, propped upright on a couch by an aunt on either side.

'To Jack and Jill!' he cried, waving an empty glass. 'And when they go up the hill, may they fetch back something stronger than water!'

Jack stood up, and the room went round; but it couldn't have been his head because that was as steady as a house. With careful steps and guiding hand, he moved among a maze of chairs and a garden of feet, filling up glasses that winked like dew.

'No more for me, dear,' murmured an aunt, putting a hand

over her glass, but so late that sherry went up her sleeve, and she gave a little scream.

Paper rustled; everyone watched.

'No present like the time!' shouted Uncle Goodman, quick as a flash, as Jill unwrapped a clock like a marble tomb.

Either by chance or design, the hands were set at half-past twelve, and everybody exclaimed over the happy idea. The toast went round for half-past twelve on Sunday, and joyful days and nights; and the vicar declared it to be the time of the singing of birds, and the voice of the turtle is heard in our land, and the youngest bridesmaid looked at him as if she thought he'd gone off his head.

At last the presents began to dwindle, not only in number but in size and importance. There was a mustard-pot, probably plated, a salt-cellar, an ivory paper-knife with a silver handle, and six little coffee spoons interred in black velvet, like ladles that had died in infancy. And then there was something else.

'That's strange,' said Jill, whisking back her hair as if it had confused her eyes. 'Here's something addressed just to Jack!'

She held out a brown paper parcel, done up in a roll. Jack took it, and stared at it. The postmark was unreadable; the writing, spidery and unknown. He felt a sudden chill, as if someone had walked on his grave.

'What is it, my boy?' asked Uncle Goodman, with a wink like an eclipse of the sun. 'Something from your shady past?'

Jack smiled foolishly, and for once could think of no humorous reply. The parcel troubled him. Although it was perfectly plain it must have been a wedding-present, for it had come to the Goodmans' house, he did not want to open it. He could not say why.

'Don't keep us in suspense,' persisted Uncle Goodman. 'Let's all see your guilty secret!'

What guilty secret? He had done no murder, betrayed no love, not stolen anything since he'd been a child, and then only pennies and sweets. Yet as he sat there, holding the parcel, he had a

8

sudden, ridiculous hope that a wind would come from nowhere and whisk the mysterious gift into the fire.

'Go on, Jack, open it,' urged Jill with a curious smile: and he wondered, fleetingly, if it could contain a gift from her to him. Then he remembered, she was giving him cuff-links . . . .

He felt eyes fixed upon him expectantly. He looked up, and saw unnaturally large faces with unnaturally large smiles. Everything seemed to have changed. He glanced at the sideboard, and the self-important teapots, attended by the squat toadies of cream jugs, seemed threatening, like policemen . . . .

He shivered; and tore open the parcel. Within was a plain cardboard tube. He shook it; and, with trembling fingers, drew out a roll of parchment, such as might have been used to make a lampshade. He opened it out. It was a map.

He could have shouted with relief! God knew what he'd been expecting; but then there are guilty shadows in every mind, and dark, unwholesome thoughts. But it was only a map!

What a strange gift, and nothing to say who had sent it. He searched the wrapping-paper, he peered through the cardboard tube, and saw Uncle Goodman, glowing like the planet Mars; and there was no card or message anywhere. It must have been forgotten . . . .

The map was old, and drawn by hand. It represented what could have been a coastline, with a narrow shore and trees beyond, a whole forest of them. But there was no scale to show whether it was a county or a continent; and no words to explain if it was China or the Isle of Man. Compass points were given, but only for North and South. They were indicated by two arrows in a circle, oddly like a clock set at half-past twelve.

He did not know where it was, yet it was strangely familiar, like a thought at the back of his mind.

'Where is it?' he heard voices murmur. 'Where can it be?' Hands reached out, and the map was passed round the room. Everybody fancied they knew it, even remembered the splutter of a mapping pen as they'd traced it at school. It was the River Jordan;

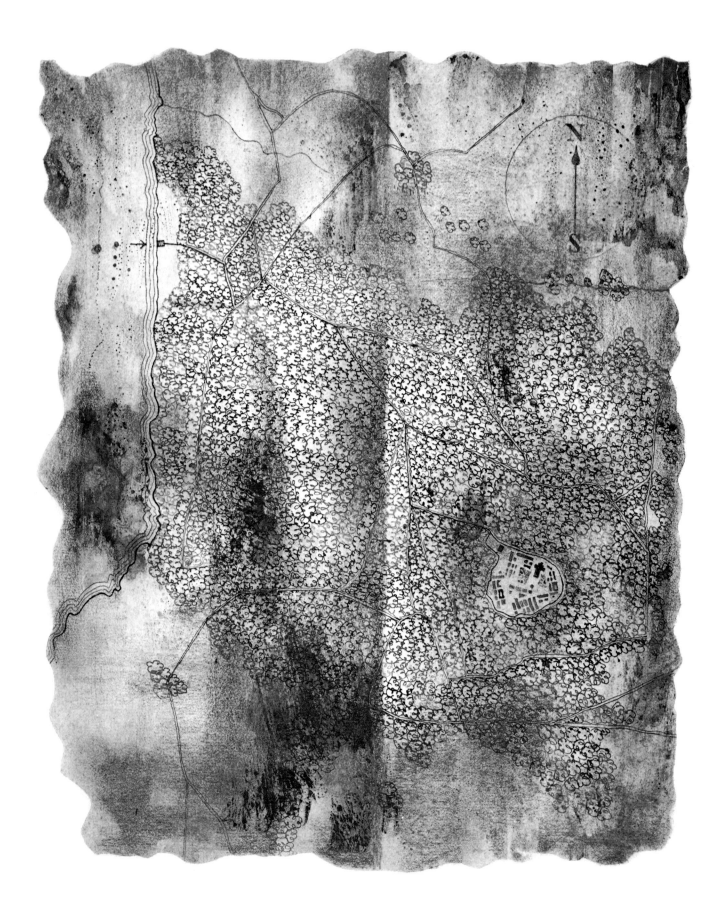

it was the coast of Cyprus; it was the Tigris, and there was Baghdad; or it was the River Rhine, and the trees depicted one of those gloomy forests, so dear to the Brothers Grimm. An atlas was fetched, to put an end to speculation; but it did no such thing. The map fitted nowhere, save, obstinately, at the back of the mind.

At length, the fire burned low in the grate and the wind complained in the chimney, as if it was feeling the chill. The atlas was put away and the quest abandoned, for it was late and time to go.

Outside the mist had thickened and muffled the porch-lamp of the Goodmans' house, so that it shone like a faint chrysanthemum of light.

'Till Sunday at half-past twelve, my darling,' murmured Jill.

'Don't be long, dear,' came her mother's voice. 'The night air's damp, and you'll catch a chill.'

'It seems so long to wait,' said Jack, 'till Sunday at half-past twelve.'

'You'll be seeing more than enough of each other after Sunday,' called Uncle Goodman. 'Come inside and shut the door!'

There was silence, and Jill's face filled up the universe, as they kissed each other good-night. Then Jack walked away down the drive and turned into the darkness of the lane.

He did not look back. He felt the house was watching him. His heart was beating rapidly, and his forehead was like ice. He had done a stupid thing. He had taken away the map. He'd slipped it into his pocket while nobody was looking. Why? He couldn't understand how he had come to do such a thing. He turned up his coat collar and ran like a thief.

He had been meaning to get it framed, of course! That was why he had taken it! He must have suffered a rush, not of blood, but of sherry, to the head, and the idea had just tumbled off a shelf in his brain.

This comforting explanation occurred to him as he was sitting in the railway carriage on his way back to London. He felt so

11

pleased with himself for having thought of it that he beamed round at the other passengers. They either buried their faces in newspapers, or looked apprehensive, as if they expected him to do something outrageous, like being sick or bursting into song.

As it happened, a song did float into his mind, and he couldn't help humming it to himself, and waving his hand and nodding his head in time:

'O mistress mine! where are you roaming?
O! stay and hear; your true love's coming ....'

He couldn't remember any more, apart from:

'Journeys end in lovers meeting.'

He thought again about the map, not that it had ever been out of his thoughts. He wondered idly if it was worth bringing it out on the off-chance that there was a professor of geography in the carriage. He studied his fellow-passengers intently, for signs of unusual scholarship; but found none. He turned away and regarded his own reflection in the window. He was shocked to see how wild and brooding his eyes looked! And his face was covered with tears! No. It had been raining and the whole window was grief-stricken. He tried to watch the dark landscape as it whirled past, but the mist muffled everything.

14

It was thicker than ever in London. The ghostly bridal veil that had hung over the woods and fields of Hertfordshire had become quite a blanket, as if it had been thought best to hide the bride completely, lest the bridegroom fly in terror. Before Sunday at half-past twelve!

He bit his lip. The thought seemed to have slipped into his head while he wasn't looking. He glanced up at the station clock. It gave a feverish little jerk and pointed, he was relieved to see, to twenty minutes to ten; and thereafter remained in a state of motionless suspension. Perhaps it had stopped? He took out the map and consulted it, as if it was a watch. Half-past twelve, said the compass points.

He shook his head. He'd better walk home instead of taking a taxi. He needed to clear his brain. He left the station and began to walk up Pentonville Road, towards his home in Islington. After about ten minutes he became aware that the buildings were wrong. He was not in Pentonville Road at all. He was in Gray's Inn Road, and walking rapidly and purposefully towards Holborn and the City.

He stopped, meaning to turn back. But why should he? There was no one waiting for him; and it was pleasant to walk by night. He nodded, as if a companion, and not himself, had, for some secret reason, persuaded him.

He walked on. The fog was nowhere so dense as to be

uncomfortable. He could quite easily see a dozen or more yards ahead, before everything became vague and indistinct; and there was no doubt that walking was doing him good. Already he'd remembered another line of the song:

'Trip no further, pretty sweeting ....'

He paused under a street-lamp that enveloped him in a misty yellow light.

'But I won't trip,' he said to himself, 'if I walk carefully.' He laughed at his own little joke: and someone passing, turned to stare.

He was on a corner. Across the road he could just make out an elderly building, with a witch-like, gingerbread air. It seemed to have a broken back, and was leaning heavily on crutches. It could have been Staple Inn. He walked towards it. There was a jeweller's shop nearby, with a clock hanging up outside, like an enormous biscuit-tin with hands. It said, a quarter to one, and had done so for years. It was stone-dead; but at least it was right twice in every twenty-four hours, which was more than could be claimed for the living!

He peered in the jeweller's window, and saw tray upon tray of wedding-rings – enough to marry a whole townful! They had steel bars in front, as if to protect them from plundering grooms and desperate brides –

'Can I be of assistance, sir?'

Most mysteriously, a policeman was standing beside him, steaming gently, like a coffee-pot with buttons. He seemed to have eyes that worked independently, as one was fixed upon Jack, and the other on the jeweller's window.

'No . . . no, thank you,' Jack muttered; and then remembered what his old nurse had always told him: 'If you want to know anything, Jack, just ask a policeman, dear. They always know.'

'Do you know where this is?' he asked, holding out the map.

The policeman examined it cautiously; and shook his head.

'Looks like,' he said, 'Captain Kidd's map of his treasure.' He chuckled. 'More in a sailor's line, I should say. You want to try around the docks, sir.'

He would indeed! It was an excellent idea! He thanked the policeman warmly, and left him, a smudge in the fog.

He walked on into the City, along Cheapside, and Poultry, and Leadenhall Street, between monstrous Banks, and gigantic Building Societies, and Mutual Provident Friendly Associations, and granite-faced Trusts, that looked as if they'd never trusted anyone in their lives. They loomed and threatened on every side, and seemed to be eyeing the fog speculatively, as if wondering how it might be turned into money. Here and there, between them, pale grey churches with humbled spires, cowered down, as if they'd been taken into custody.

There wasn't a soul about. He could have dropped down dead and no one would have known.

'"O mistress mine!"' he sang, to keep up his spirits, '"where are you roaming?"'

Not in Leadenhall Street, and that was for certain sure!

'"O! stay and hear; your true love's coming ...."'

But only if he could find the way! He took out the map yet again and stared at it, as if by constant looking, it would yield up its secret. But it remained as mysterious and haunting as ever. He put it away and hastened on; for the strange feeling it always communicated to him, was growing stronger and stronger ....

Presently, the grim City was no more than a gloomy bulk behind him, and he passed down endless mean streets of tattered shops, that seemed to be selling what nobody wanted, and dreary houses with bleary, yellow eyes, that seemed to watch his progress enviously .... He supposed he must be somewhere in Whitechapel, or Stepney, or even further east; that is, if he was still walking east .... He began stopping passers-by:

'Please can you tell me the way to the docks?'

'Which docks?'

'Just the docks ... any docks.'

Sometimes he was answered by no more than a shrug; sometimes he was obliged with directions so complicated that he couldn't possibly hold them in his brain. Whenever a face looked helpful, he held out the map and asked:

'Do you know where this is?'

But the night was full of shaking heads. He lingered by public houses with frost-embroidered windows, glimmering grandly on corners, and breathing forth blasts of beery air and raucous song. But those who came out could scarcely find the pavement, let alone see the map that was held out in front of them, with the question that was becoming more and more urgent as the night went on.

'Do you know where this is?'

He had to find out! It was the most important thing in his life. He had to find out because, in his heart of hearts, he knew he must go there. And before Sunday at half-past twelve. Otherwise it would be too late.

That was the strange feeling that the map had always communicated to him, and had driven him on through the night. It was almost as if he had an appointment to keep ....

The fog was much thicker now. The air smelled riverish and the streets had turned narrow and steep. He kept catching glimpses of huge, threatening gates, and gaunt cranes, grazing hopelessly over wastelands of rubbish, as if for worms. He must have been very near the river, as he could hear water, muttering and sighing.

He saw a faint stain of coloured light in the air, and walked towards it. It turned into a small public house, standing forlornly by itself, as if all the other houses had crept away while it had been asleep. It was very old, and very dirty, with stained-glass windows, like an unfrocked church. It was called 'The Bird-in-Hand'.

Suddenly the door opened and a shadowy figure stumbled out. It was an old man in a jersey and rubber boots. He peered about him, rubbed the fog out of his eyes and called out:

'Charlie! Are you there, Charlie?'

He caught sight of Jack, and came towards him sideways, as if prepared, any moment, to run off.

'You ain't seen Charlie, have you?'

'Who's Charlie?'

'Me grandson. About your height, about your age, I should say.'

'No. I'm sorry. I haven't seen anyone.'

The old man scratched his head and scowled into the fog.

They were standing by one of the windows. Jack took out the map and held it under the grimy light.

'Do you know where this is?'

The old man peered at it, then looked straight at Jack.

'Yes,' he said. 'I know.'

Jack trembled with excitement, and almost with fear. At last! 'Where? Where is it?'

'In yer 'and!' said the old man, and straightaway doubled himself up into a hoop of horrible laughter. 'In yer 'and, in yer 'and!'

Tears rushed into Jack's eyes, tears of bitterness and hatred and unutterable despair –

'Don't 'it me!' pleaded the old man, between gusts. 'Don't 'it me! I'm only an old man! Charlie! Charlie! Come and 'elp me, for Gawd's sake!'

'What is it, grand-dad?'

Half a young man had risen up, seemingly from the dark river itself. It was Charlie. He finished climbing the stone steps and came towards his grandfather with a stern expression on his face.

'What's the old rogue been up to?' he asked Jack.

'It was nothing.'

'That's right!' said the old man eagerly. ''e asked me about 'is map. That's all, Charlie, on me honour. 'e wanted to know where it was . . . and I was goin' to tell 'im, only first I 'ad to 'ave me little joke – '

'Let's have a look at it,' said Charlie, holding out his hand. He took it and looked at it carefully. Then he gave it back.

'Do – do you know where it is?'

'Yes.'

'Then – then where?'

'About two hours down the river, allowing for wind and tide.'

'As near as that!'

'Where did you think it was? In darkest Africa, or something?'

'How can I get there?'

'Come with us, if you like. The tide's on the turn, and we're sailing now.'

Their vessel rode gently against the steps, which vanished into the water, and was moored to an iron ring in the river wall. It was a barge with a single mast and a huge and ghostly sail. There was a lantern at the mast-head, another at the stern, and a third overhanging the bows; so that, as Charlie pushed off, and the barge began to move, it seemed like a constellation of stars, winking and swinging through the densely swirling night.

Charlie took the tiller and his grandfather leaned over the prow, like an ugly figure-head, to scare away birds and ghosts.

'Don't pay no heed to his tales,' called out Charlie, 'of Flying Dutchmen in the Sargasso, and sea-serpents round the Cape of Storms. He's never been further than Tilbury in his life; and no more have I.'

The old man screwed up his face in resentment; and then

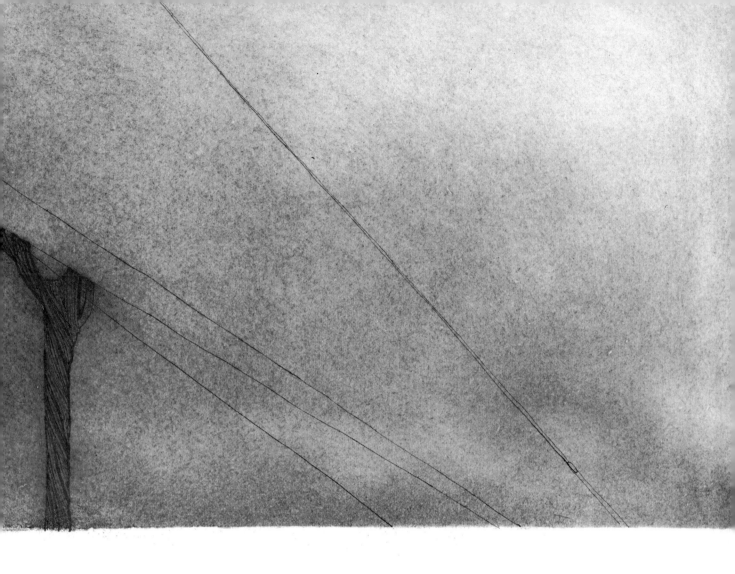

contented himself with singing dreadful sea-shanties, in a high, squeezed-out voice, that must have struck terror into the hearts of the other river folk, who could see neither the barge nor the screechy old man. Presently Charlie joined him, in a sturdy baritone that was as sonorous as an organ in its lowest notes; while Jack, his heart beating wildly, leaned against the side and stared and stared into the phantoms of the fog.

> 'O! stay and hear; your true love's coming.
> That can sing both high and low.'

he remembered, as the weirdly melodious barge sailed on, shrill and deep.

Suddenly the whole circumstance of where he was, and where

he was going, seemed impossible and utterly unreal. He was dreaming it. The barge he was standing on was not real, even though he could feel every roughness and indentation of the wood against which he leaned; Charlie and his grandfather were not real, even though he could see the steamy puffs of breath that came out of the old man's mouth as he sang, and catch whiffs of beer and pickled onions that kept coming off him in waves.

He must have dozed off at some time in the night, and was locked in this strange dream. He tried to think back, to fix on the exact moment when it had begun. Perhaps it had been at the Goodmans' house, and at any moment he would wake up out of a sherry-dream, with Uncle Goodman bellowing out some stupid joke about sleeping the sleep of the just after.

But what if the Goodmans' house itself had been a dream?

26

What if he had dreamed the wedding-rehearsal, the top hat and the lavender coat with a tail, the carnations in silver socks and the teapots and toast-racks on the sideboard? What if Jill herself, and Uncle Goodman, and even Samuel Best the Builders' Merchant, were a dream from which he had awakened at some time in the night?

'Uncle Goodman!' he called out loudly.

'Wake up,' said the old man. 'There's no Uncle Goodman 'ere. You're on the river, me lad, with Charlie and 'is grand-dad!'

He shook his head and smiled ruefully. Whichever way round, it was better to be wisely asleep than foolishly awake.

On and on sailed the barge, with the water rushing softly past the bows, and the great sail grunting as it shifted and strained.

Sometimes the fog thinned sufficiently to afford glimpses of barges moored together, like floating islands, and of faint lights gleaming on the river's banks; but mostly it was a very secret journey, with the fog often obscuring even Charlie and the old man.

About two hours, Charlie had said, allowing for wind and tide; but time on the river seemed to run differently from time on land. It might have been one hour, or even four, when at last the sail was lowered and the barge was bumping gently against a jetty, to which it was secured by a rope round a bollard.

'Are we here?' whispered Jack. He was suddenly frightened at the thought of what might be awaiting him. And worst of all, was a dread that it might be nothing.

'We're 'ere,' said the old man. 'It's you what's there!' And he pointed to a flight of stone stairs.

'Careful how you go,' warned Charlie, as Jack climbed over the side. 'Them stairs are slippery.'

Jack mounted the steps, slowly and cautiously. By the time he had reached the top, Charlie had cast off and hoisted the sail. Already the barge was beginning to move away. He watched its lanterns swinging and dwindling, and its great sail melting into the fog. Then he remembered something he hadn't taken into account. Instantly he was filled with alarm. He waved and shouted:

'How do I get back?'

The old man almost fell into the river with laughing.

'You should 'ave thought on that,' came the faint answer, 'when you was back at The Bird-in-'and!'

Then the fog swirled and the barge dissolved, leaving behind only an imprint on the memory. Last seen were its lanterns, like three stars that blinked … and went out.

He was alone. For some minutes he remained standing where he was, half-hoping for the barge to return; then he turned his back on the river and began to walk.

He had not gone more than twenty yards before he noticed that the fog was thinning quite rapidly, and that the air itself was becoming lighter. The journey down-river must have taken considerably longer than he'd guessed; for he saw, with surprise, that the sky was already pale with dawn.

He stopped and took out the map and studied it. Then he gazed about him. Although it was not possible to make out the line of the river, as it was still heavily obscured, he could see that where he was corresponded exactly with the map. The narrow shore turned out to be an area of sand, beyond which grew the trees. As far as he could see, in either direction, the sand was empty and unbroken. There was no one about, and no sound, save the occasional shriek of a lonely sea-bird.

He stared towards the trees. They were dark and quiet. He could not see how far they stretched, but it seemed to be for a great distance. It was a forest.

He took out the map and looked at it yet again. As he did so, he knew that it was to be for the last time. He stared at it, until every detail was fixed in his mind as clearly as his own name. Then he put it away and set off across the sand towards the trees. He knew, whatever it was that he must discover, whatever strange appointment he was to keep, it lay somewhere in the dark forest.

31

He walked with breathless excitement, and great watchfulness. Every bush, every thicket, every sudden congregation of shadows might have concealed what he had come to find.

He had entered the forest at a point where there had appeared to be a path, and had followed it thereafter. At times, it had seemed almost wide enough to have been a drive, although it was always soft underfoot with rotting leaves and moss, and betrayed no sign of gravel ever having been there. Nonetheless, it was curious that no trees seemed to have encroached upon it, though they grew profusely everywhere else.

At first, it had been quite light. The morning had leaked through the forest's roof in a thousand places, and made a bright patchwork of brown and green, with, here and there, the delicate trunks of birches showing up like silvery inscriptions. But very soon, the branches had arched more closely overhead, and the forest had become sombre and dim.

Although it was November, and the day before had been cold, he felt so warm from walking, that he had to take off his coat. For a little way, he carried it over his arm; but the thorny undergrowth that had begun to invade the path, kept catching at it. At length, he shrugged his shoulders, and hung it up on a branch.

'Stay there,' he said, with an air of careless bravado he was far from feeling, 'until I come back for you.' Then a sombre thought struck him. 'And if I don't, well, it won't matter, will it!'

He tried to forget about his coat, and had almost succeeded, when a most curious circumstance brought it back sharply into the front of his mind. The path had become more and more tangled with sharp bushes, and, as he pushed his way onward, he began to notice that what appeared to be dead blossoms were clinging to overhanging branches. He was so struck by the variety of colours, that he stopped to examine them more closely. They were not blossoms, but fragments of clothing. It would seem that other coats had been hung in the forest, and moths of time had feasted on them.

He frowned uneasily, but continued on his way. He was filled

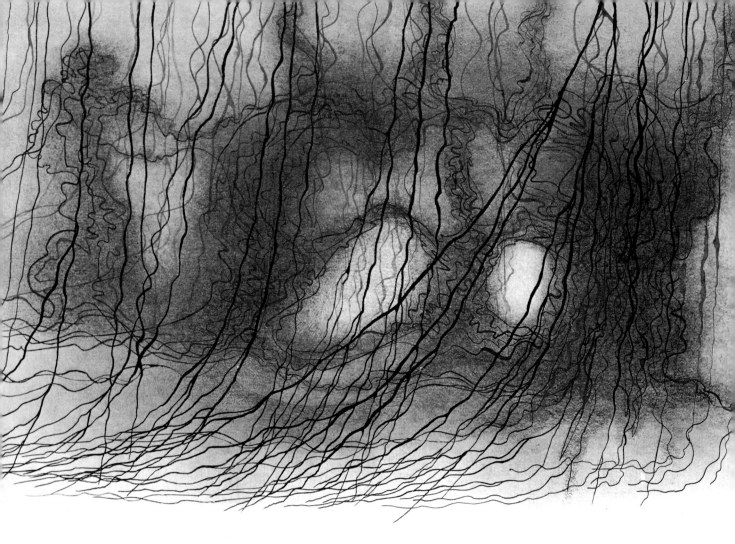

with so strong a sense of curiosity and adventure, that nothing seemed able to deter him. His only regret was, that he was not wearing tremendous leather thigh-boots, as his respectable trousers were becoming fragmentary, from the continual plucking of sly thorns.

'And a sword,' he added, 'to cut my way through. Or at least something better than a ridiculous pocket-knife with folding scissors that won't even cut paper.'

The way through the forest had now become quite dense, and the path was difficult to distinguish. The trees on either side had begun to assume fantastic shapes, as they turned and twisted in their efforts to find light. Sometimes they looked exactly like horribly hooped old men, with gnarled arms outstretched, as if for money. It was a forest of cripples and menacing beggars, who kept trying to scratch his eyes out.

The strange, coloured blossoms had been left behind; and in

34

their place were tiny, white buds that speckled the undergrowth like frost-needles, or snowflakes. Whenever he brushed against them, they tumbled to the ground.

At first, he could not imagine what they were; but, as he stumbled on, they became larger and more distinct, so that it was no longer possible to mistake them. They were bones.

He saw ribs, sometimes three or four together, like toast-racks; he saw fingers and toes, scattered like pale confetti on the ground. He saw a skull, lodged among thorns. Twigs were growing out of its sockets, like weirdly glamorous eyelashes. It grinned and nodded as the bush was disturbed, and seemed to say:

'Journey's end . . . journey's end . . . .'

He stopped, cold with fear. He stared about him. There was another skull, grinning at him from the branches of a hornbeam; and below it, lay its thousand separate belongings – ribs, teeth, toes and fingers – in a pallid heap.

35

Filled with horror and dread, he pushed aside a tangle of briars and brambles. He cried out. The forest was everywhere alive with death! Bony grinners glimmered from hollies and hawthorns, and, deep in thickets, whole skeletons danced gently, and shed their fingers like greyish-white gloves.

What had happened in this terrible place so long, long ago? Was it a graveyard, a plague-pit, that the growing forest had disturbed, and thrust up above the ground? Or was it the place of some ancient battlefield that time had disinterred?

Either explanation was possible, and might have been the truth. Except for one strange thing. Every single skull was facing the same way. They were all grinning – at him!

Desperately he tried to push on; but he could go no further. A wall of branches confronted him, and he could see no way round.

'Journey's end … journey's end ….' mocked the pale watchers; and their grins seemed to grow broader, as terror seized him, and bitter dismay!

Was this really journey's end? Was this what he had come so far to find? Was he like the merchant in the old story who, unknowingly, kept an appointment with Death?

Furiously he grasped the branches, and shook them with all his might. Ribs and thigh-bones and skulls came tumbling down upon him in a dreadful hail. They struck him on the arms, the shoulders and the head, as if in a futile effort to beat him back. But still he shook and pushed at the wall of branches. Then, suddenly, the wall moved; and with a loud, harsh groan, the whole forest seemed to open before him!

His way had been barred by gates, by a pair of tall, wrought-iron gates, that had been completely overgrown. Beyond, he saw grass, but grown so tall that it was like an immense green curtain, through which bright sunshine gleamed. The air was warm, and very still.

A feeling of enormous relief overwhelmed him, and his eyes filled with tears. His journey had not yet ended! Suddenly his heart and head were full of the music and words of the song. He longed

to sing it aloud, for he had remembered how it went on:

> 'What is love? 'tis not hereafter;
> Present mirth hath present laughter.
> What's to come is *still* unsure ....'

Eagerly he passed through the gates; and behind him in the forest, glimmering from bramble and hawthorn, from holly-bush and briar, the skulls continued to grin with bony mirth and bony, silent laughter.

So quiet was the world beyond the gates, that it was as if the morning had raised its finger to its lips, warning him to walk softly, and upon tiptoe, and to walk carefully, for the rustling of the tall grass was much too loud.

Brighter and brighter grew the sunlight, until every blade seemed edged with gold. At last the green curtain thinned and parted; and the landscape was revealed. Jack stood still, scarcely daring to breathe. The prospect before him was one of strange splendour.

On gently rising ground stood a mansion of soft, yellow stone,

a stately mansion with towers and turrets, and a hundred windows that blazed with the sun. From the centre of the building rose a gilded clock-tower. The hands of the clock pointed to half-past twelve. It was journey's end.

He began to walk forward, slowly and wonderingly. The mansion was approached by wide, terraced lawns, smooth as green table-cloths, and gravelled walks that were queerly peopled, here and there, by gossiping groups of box trees, in the dark shapes of peacocks, vases, pagodas and gigantic pineapples, such as no trees, even in their wildest dreams, would have assumed of their own accord.

He passed an ornamental lake, bright and still as a looking-glass, in which stood four carved children, holding up four carved fishes, as if, long ago, they had been caught poaching, and had been punished by being turned into stone.

He passed quaintly shaped flower-beds, gorgeous with roses, carnations, pinks and sweet-williams, like enormous bouquets. Yet it was November, and yesterday had been cold.

It was quiet everywhere, very quiet. Nothing ruffled the surface of the lake, and the flowers might have been painted, for there was no scent in the air. Nothing moved, nothing stirred, save

Jack and his black shadow, as he began to mount the steps that led towards the mansion's great front door.

He kept looking up towards the windows, and shading his eyes against their glare. But no face appeared in any of them; and the front door remained shut.

He felt small and lonely, and uncertain; and he became uncomfortably aware of how unsuitable was his appearance. His clothing was torn, his hair was wild, and his hands and face were grimy from the forest. What should he do when he reached the door and knocked? What should he say when it was answered?

He mounted the last step, and, as he did so, his foot caught against something that fell with a clatter. He looked down. He had knocked over some quaint, wooden toy that had been left outside. He bent to pick it up; and saw that it was not a toy at all. It was an old-fashioned spinning-wheel.

He set it upright, and tried to turn the wheel; but it was stiff with age. He looked at the spindle. Curiously he touched it. It was as sharp as a thorn and the tip was darkly stained, as if, long ago, some careless spinner had pricked herself . . . .

He stood up. Strange dreams and memories stirred in his mind; and he felt as cold as ice. He looked back, over the quiet gardens, the breathless flowers, the still lake, and the uncanny summer that lay, like a golden dream over the silent house.

He stared at the heavy oaken door, with its great brass knocker, like a lion's head; and he knew that there was no purpose in knocking. If he knocked till kingdom-come, no one would answer that door. If he shouted with all his might, no one would hear his voice.

His heart thundered as all the shadowy feelings that had haunted and tantalized him, and driven him on, sprang out into the bright light of day! At last he knew where he was, and who he was. He had come to the palace of the Sleeping Beauty, and he was the prince who was to awaken her!

He pushed at the door. It opened, quietly. He stepped inside. Everything was dark, and smelled of dust and sleep. He paused to listen; and fancied that the mansion itself was breathing, gently and softly. The air of secrecy was almost suffocating.

He moved towards the nearest door, and his feet sank ankle-deep in dust. He opened it and looked into the room. Someone was sitting at a table, under a shawl of dust. He looked into another room. Three figures lay on the floor, huddled up like frightened hedgehogs; but whether they were men or women was impossible to say. Thick, grey dust covered them from head to foot.

He went into other rooms. He walked noiselessly along passages and through great galleries, where proud pictures looked serenely down. He peered into small parlours and summer-rooms, and kitchens, pantries and stone sculleries ... and everywhere, in chairs, on benches and on tiled floors, lay sleepers, wrapped in thick cocoons of dust, like enormous, unborn moths.

Some had been prepared for what had overtaken them, and lay on couches and divans, in the seemly attitudes of sleep; but

others had been taken unawares. One had been writing a letter, another had been drinking wine, and the bottle was overturned; and yet another had been vainly combing her hair, and leaned, with her head upon a dressing-table, and the tilted mirror dimly reflecting a face made of dust.

He saw a velvety grey cushion on a chair, rising and falling as the cat within dozed on and on, in the longest catnap ever; and dreaming of – of what? He wondered what they could all have been dreaming of, for so long? Or had their sleep been a blank?

He went upstairs, and the broad balustrade discharged grey fog into the hall as he mounted. He went into bedroom after bedroom, seeking everywhere for the Sleeping Beauty.

At last only one room remained to be searched. It was reached by a winding stairway that led to a turret, high up in the mansion. The door lay open, as if someone had been long expected.

Breathlessly, Jack went inside. The room was circular, and there were windows all round, through which sunlight floated faintly, like a golden cobweb. In the middle of the room, stood a four-poster bed. He crept towards it; and then stood, and stared down upon the Sleeping Beauty.

So this was she, a quietly breathing greyness that had neither shape nor form! There was a table beside the bed, and on it, he could just make out that there was a book. Curiously he picked it up and wiped it clean. It was a diary. He turned the pages. They were all blank.

He put it back and knelt down beside the shrouded sleeper. Gently he reached out and touched the dust that covered her face. Then he drew his hand away, and flesh gleamed softly where his fingers had rested. He wiped her brow, and discovered a milky-white calmness underneath. Softly, and with infinite care, he blew upon her eyes, and revealed delicately veined lids, that seemed to quiver, and long, dark lashes. He brushed her cheeks, and a rosy blush showed through the grey. He stroked her hair, and, little by little, unravelled bright gold from under the drab bridal veil of time. Last of all he mined for rubies, and wiped away the dust from her lips. They were full and soft, and seemed to be smiling.

He stood back, and gazed in wonderment at what he had uncovered, and his heart ached with longing.

He must kiss her! It was his plain duty. That was how the tale went. 'And then, Jack dear, the prince woke her with a kiss, and they lived happily ever after!'

He smiled; he beamed. He wondered how it would be when her eyes opened. What would be their colour? Pleasurably he imagined them widening in surprise, and then gleaming with delight as she beheld her long awaited prince.

Prince! Surely the title was only meant to be figurative, and referred as much to behaviour and appearance, as to birth.

Appearance! His heart sank. He went to the dressing-table

and polished the mirror with the sleeve of his jacket. He looked at himself. He was more like an overgrown street-urchin than a prince, figurative or otherwise. If she opened her eyes on such a sight as he saw in the mirror, she might well close them again, for another hundred years.

Anxiously he attempted to restore order to his hair, and to wipe away the worst of the forest's dirt from his face. At length he returned to kneel beside the bed. He leaned forward towards the sleeper's lips.

'Do you know the old song?' he whispered.

> '"What's to come is still unsure:
>   In delay there lies no plenty ...."'

Yet he did delay. A host of doubts and fears and guilty thoughts had suddenly assailed him. He was about to betray one love for another. What of Jill, whom he loved dearly? What of the wedding and all the world and his wife who were coming to celebrate the marriage?

He felt unbearably wretched. He drew back from the sleeper, and tears were running down his face. He knew that he must go back, and that the Sleeping Beauty must sleep on, for another hundred years.

He bit his lip. He wanted desperately to kiss her, and awaken her. The rest of his life, the Goodmans, Samuel Best the Builders' Merchant, and all domestic prosperity, seemed like heavy chains about his soul. He must break them! No matter what effort it cost, no matter what pain it caused, he must be free!

> 'In delay there lies no plenty;
>   Then come kiss me, sweet and twenty ....'

Sweet and twenty! A generous estimate to be sure! Though she did not look a day above eighteen, she must have been a hundred years more than that at the very least! He smiled. He would never

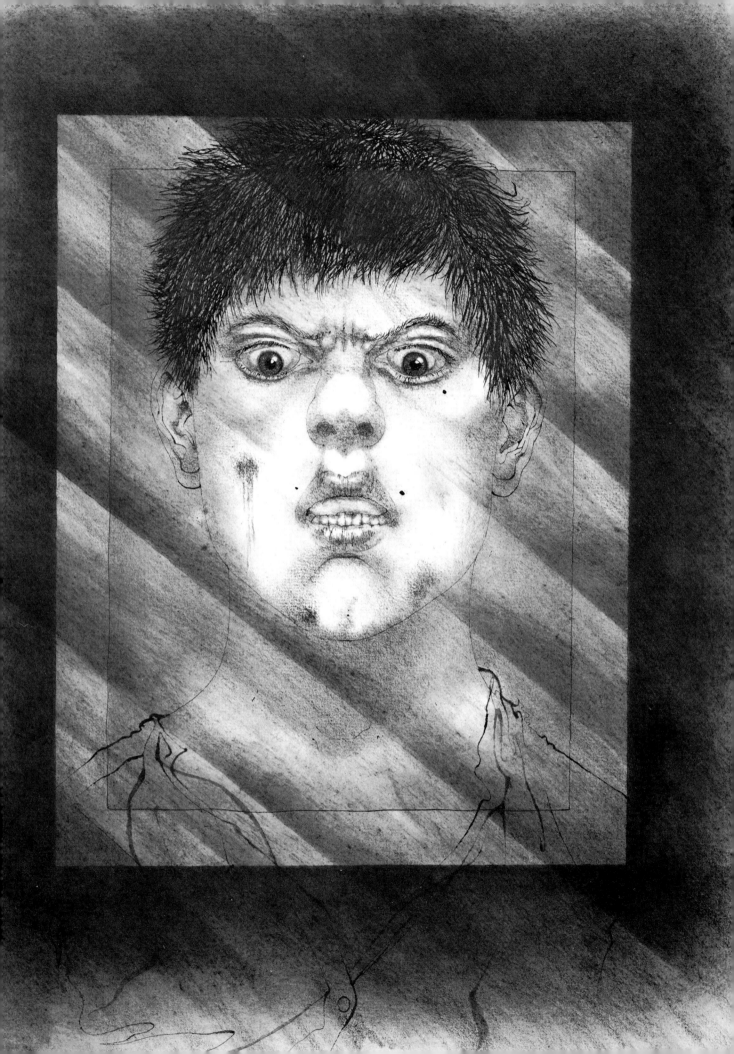

breathe a word of it. He would be too much a gentleman to remind a lady of her age!

'Then come kiss me, sweet and twenty,
Youth's a stuff will not endure.'

Again he hesitated, as new fears invaded him. '"Youth's a stuff will not endure,"' he repeated. No more would she! Once awakened, she like all the world, would be a slave to Time, and would grow old. The leaves would fall, the flowers in the enchanted garden would wither and die, the mansion itself would crumble, and the marvellous summer that lay dreaming over the little world, would be no more. 'And then, Jack dear, the prince woke her up with a kiss, and they lived – ' He shook his head.

She was not for him. Filled with a deep sadness and an infinite regret, he turned away from the bed. He must leave the room; he must leave the sleeping mansion as he had found it. He must cross the quiet gardens once more, and go back through the iron gates, as silently as if he himself was no more than a shadowy dream, that had come, and gone away. He must return through the dark forest . . . .

The forest. The thought of it filled him with dread. The skulls and skeletons glimmering in brambles and thickets would be awaiting him. But at least he would be spared their mocking, bony grins. They had all been looking towards him as he had approached as if –

Suddenly he understood why! He struggled to avoid the truth; but he could not. He stared round the room. He fancied he could make out, under the carpet of dust that lay on the floor, a host of phantom footprints, approaching to the bed, and then retreating back through the door.

So he was not the first prince to have found the mansion and gazed down upon the Sleeping Beauty. Many another had been there before him, had stood where he now stood; and, for one reason or another, had sadly gone away.

They had gone back through the forest; and there they remained, strangled by branches, and stabbed by thorns. They had all perished; not a single one had escaped.

It was death either way; it was death to go, death to stay. He went back to the bed, and knelt beside it.

"'Then come kiss me, sweet and twenty!'" he whispered; and the last line was lost in her lips, and in the opening of her marvellous eyes.

She tasted of toast and honey, and he was enormously relieved! In his heart of hearts he had dreaded that she would have tasted of dust. But it was toast and honey; as if that was what she had been thinking of when she'd fallen asleep, and had been dreaming of it for a hundred years!

'Oh!' she said; and thereafter there was such an explosion of happenings that Jack no more knew what came after or what came before; which was night, which was day; whether it was still yesterday, or the middle of next week; which was her father, which was her cat; which was the butler, which was the rose-garden, than, as the saying goes, a kipper knows of Yarmouth!

'Oh!' said the princess; and Time, which had been asleep for so long that it had got out of the habit of minutes and hours and days, woke up and bundled them all together anyhow!

There was such a barking of clocks and a striking of dogs, such an uproar of sneezes and feet; there was such a rushing and rustling and crowding in of faces, and shaking of dusty hands and kissing of dusty cheeks, that his thoughts flew into as many bright pieces as a broken mirror.

'Oh!' said the princess; and nothing more.

Her voice had been low and soft, and he longed to hear her speak; but there never seemed to be time. So much to be done, so much to be done before the wedding!

He caught a glimpse of her in the rose-garden, then her ladies-in-waiting crowded round, like enormous tea-cosies. He saw her on the stairs. She smiled and waved; and her mother called. He saw her sitting by the lake, gazing into the water; but he was with the tailor, the hatter, the bootmaker, the barber, the Bishop's chaplain, and a gentleman from the *Gazette*; and he might as well have been in chains.

He saw her a hundred times, through windows, across galleries, along passages; but always either he or she was with someone else, and there was never time for more than a nod and a smile and a wave.

He treasured them up in his heart, her nods, her waves, her smiles, her taste of toast and honey, and her softly surprised, 'Oh!'

'Time enough after the wedding,' everybody told him. 'Now you must visit here; and she must go there . . . . '

After the wedding was all he had to hope for, after the wedding he would know his bride.

They were to be married on Sunday at half-past twelve. It was in a cathedral, no less: a huge mountain of a church that was all gargoyles and bishops and saints.

It was vast and dim within, with dead kings and dead heroes, lying in little marble prisons around the walls. Everywhere there were tall grey pillars soaring upward, like silver birches, and branching out into delicate traceries, against a stone sky.

As he walked down the aisle towards the great altar, that gleamed and glowed like a king's ransom, there was a whispering and a murmuring all round him, and programmes rustled like leaves.

At last he reached his place. Then he thought of Jill, and the Goodmans, and Samuel Best the Builders' Merchant; and he wondered what they would say if they could see him now. And his heart ached and his eyes prickled with tears.

There came a sound of shouting and cheering outside, and a rattle of wheels and a clatter of hooves. Then a townful of 'A-ahs!' and a world of, 'How beautiful!' The bride had arrived!

Every head in the tremendous congregation turned towards the door. Jack's heartache vanished, and his eyes shone. He saw a shadow cross the threshold; she was coming!

The great clock began to strike; and the organ burst forth into a stately march. The unseen player, carried away by the grandeur of the occasion, pulled out stop after stop, until the mighty instrument shouted at the top of its voice.

The altar trembled and the lofty lamps quivered and swung; but the organist played on unheeding, and the music crashed and roared.

A crack appeared in a pillar, then another and another, like black snakes writing across the grey. The altar's gorgeous vessels jumped and danced; and still the organ played.

Chains leaped from their fastenings, and lights came raining down from the dim ceiling, like flights of stars; and the very walls began to shake. The little marble prisons burst open, and the great men's bones came rattling out like dice.

The congregation rushed hither and thither, shrieking and screaming; but their voices were drowned under the organ's ceaseless roar.